Percy B. Shelley, Thomas J. Wise

Letters from Percy Bysshe Shelley to Elizabeth Hitchener

Volume 1

Percy B. Shelley, Thomas J. Wise

Letters from Percy Bysshe Shelley to Elizabeth Hitchener
Volume 1

ISBN/EAN: 9783337388096

Printed in Europe, USA, Canada, Australia, Japan

Cover: Foto ©Andreas Hilbeck / pixelio.de

More available books at **www.hansebooks.com**

LETTERS

FROM

PERCY BYSSHE SHELLEY

TO

ELIZABETH HITCHENER.

IN TWO VOLUMES.

VOL I.

1890.
London : Privately Printed.
(*Not for Sale.*)

CONTENTS.

VOL. I.

———

CONTENTS.

PAGE

ERRATUM.

Page 78.

For, *Tuesday,* 11*th November,* 1811,

Read, *Tuesday,* 12*th November,* 1811.

LETTERS.

LETTERS TO
ELIZABETH HITCHENER.

LETTER I.

FIELD PLACE,
[*Wednesday*] *June* 5, 1811.

DEAR MADAM,

I desired Locke to be sent to you from London, and the Captain has two books which he will give you—*The Curse of Kehama*, and Ensor's *National Education*. The latter is the production of a very clever man. You may keep the poem as long as you please; but I shall want the latter in the course of a month or two,—before which, however, I shall have the pleasure of seeing you.

I fear our arguments are too long, and too candidly carried on, to make any figure on paper. Feelings do not look so well as reasonings on black and white. If, however, secure of your own orthodoxy, you would attempt my proselytism, believe me I should be most happy to subject myself to the danger. But I know that you, like myself, are a devotee at the shrine of Truth. Truth is *my* God ; and say he is air, water, earth, or electricity, but I think *yours* is reducible to the same simple Divinityship. Seriously, however : if you *very* widely differ, or differ indeed in the least, from me on the subject of our late argument, the only reason which would induce me to object to a polemical correspondence is that it might deprive *your* time of that application which its value deserves : *mine* is totally vacant.

Walter Scott has published a new poem, *The Vision of Don Roderick.* I have ordered it. You shall have it when I have finished. I am not very enthusiastic in the cause of Walter Scott. The aristocratical tone which his writings assume does not prepossess me in his favour, since my opinion is that all poetical beauty ought to be subordinate to the inculcated moral,— that metaphorical language ought to be a pleasing vehicle for useful and momentous instruction. But see Ensor on the subject of poetry.

Adieu.

> Your sincere
> PERCY SHELLEY.

LETTER II.

FIELD PLACE,
[*Tuesday*] *June* 11, 1811.

MY DEAR MADAM,

With pleasure I engage in a correspondence which carries its own recommendation both with my feelings and my reason. I am now, however, an undivided votary of the latter. I do not know which were most *complimentary:* but, as you do not admire, as I do not study, this aristocratical science, it is of little consequence.

Am I to expect an enemy or an ally in Locke? Locke proves that there are no innate ideas; that, in consequence, there can be no innate speculative or practical principles,— thus overturning all appeals of *feeling* in favour of Deity, since that feeling must be referable to some origin.

There must have been a time when it did not exist; in consequence, a time when it began to exist. Since all ideas are derived from the senses, this feeling must have originated from some sensual excitation: consequently the possessor of it may be aware of the time, of the circumstances, attending its commencement. Locke proves this by induction too clear to admit of rational objection. He affirms, in a chapter of whose reasoning I leave your reason to judge, that there is a God: he affirms also, and that in a most unsupported way, that the Holy Ghost dictated St. Paul's writings. Which are we to prefer? The proof or the affirmation?

To a belief in Deity I have no objection on the score of feeling: I would as gladly, perhaps with greater pleasure, admit than doubt his existence. I now do neither: I have not the shadow of a doubt.

My wish to convince you of his
non-existence is twofold : first, on the
score of truth ; secondly, because I
conceive it to be the most summary
way of eradicating Christianity.   I
plainly tell you my intentions and my
views.   I see a being whose aim, like
mine, is virtue.   Christianity militates
with a high pursuit of it.   Hers *is* a
high pursuit of it : she is therefore not
a Christian.   Yet wherefore does she
deceive herself?   Wherefore does she
attribute to a spurious, irrational (as
proved), disjointed system of desultory
ethics,—insulting, intolerant theology,
—that high sense of calm dispassionate
virtue which her own meditations have
elicited ?   Wherefore is a man who has
profited by this error to say : " You
are regarded as a monster in society ;
eternal punishment awaits your infi-
delity ? "   " I do not believe it," is
your reply.   " Here is a book," is the
rejoinder.   " Pray to the Being who is

here described, and you shall soon believe."

Surely, if a person obstinately *wills* to believe,—determines spite of himself, spite of the refusal of that part of mind to admit the assent in which only can assent rationally be centred, —wills thus to put himself under the influence of passion,—all reasoning is superfluous. Yet I do not suppose that you *act* thus (for action it must be called, as belief is a passion); since the religion does not hold out high morality as an apology for an aberration from reason. In this latter case, reason might sanction the aberration, and fancy become but an auxiliary to its influence.

Dismiss, then, Christianity, in which no arguments can enter. Passion and Reason are in their natures opposite. Christianity is the former; and Deism (for we are now no further) is the latter.

What, then, is a "God"? It is a name which expresses the unknown cause, the suppositious origin of all existence. When we speak of the soul of man, we mean that unknown cause which produces the observable effect evinced by his intelligence and bodily animation, which are in their nature conjoined, and (as we suppose, as we observe) inseparable. The word God, then, in the sense which you take it, analogizes with the universe as the soul of man to his body; as the vegetative power to vegetables; the stony power to stones. Yet, were each of these adjuncts taken away, what would be the remainder? What is man without his soul? He is not man. What are Vegetables without their vegetative power? stones without their stony? Each of these as much constitutes the essence of men, stones, &c., as much make it what it is, as your "God" does the universe. In *this* sense I acknow-

ledge a God ; but merely as a synonym
for *the existing power of existence.*

I do not in this (nor can you do, I
think) recognize a being which has
created that to which it is confessedly
annexed as an essence, as that without
which the universe would not be what
it is. It is therefore the essence of the
universe : the universe is the essence of
it. It is another word for " the essence
of the universe." You recognize not in
this an identical being to whom are
attributable the properties of virtue,
mercy, loveliness. Imagination delights
in personification. Were it not for this
embodying quality of eccentric fancy,
we should be, to this day, without a
God. Mars was personified as the God
of War, Juno of Policy, &c.

But you have formed in your mind
the Deity of Virtue. The personification—beautiful in poetry, inadmissible
in reasoning—in the true style of
Hindoostanish devotion, you have

adopted.   I war against it for the sake
of truth.   There is such a thing as
virtue : but what, who, is this Deity of
Virtue ? Not the father of Christ, not
the source of the Holy Ghost ; not the
God who beheld with favour the coward
wretch Abraham, who built the grandeur
of his favourite Jews on the bleeding
bodies of myriads, on the subjugated
necks of the dispossessed inhabitants
of Canaan.   But here my instances
were as long as the memoir of his
furious King-like exploits, did not contempt succeed to hatred.   Did I now
see him seated in gorgeous and tyrannic
majesty, as described, upon the throne
of infinitude, if I bowed before him,
what would Virtue say ? Virtue's voice
is almost inaudible ; yet it strikes upon
the brain, upon the heart.   The howl
of self-interest is loud ; but the heart
is black which throbs solely to its note.

You say our theory is the same : I
believe it.   Then why all this ? The

power which makes me a scribbler
knows !

I have just finished a novel of the
day—*The Missionary,* by Mrs. Owenson.
It dwells on ideas which, when young,
I dwelt on with enthusiasm: now I
laugh at the weakness which is past.

The Curse of Kehama, which you will
have, is my most favourite poem ; yet
there is a great error—faith in the
character of the divine Kailyal.

Yet I forgot. I intended to mention
to you something essential. I recom-
mend reason. Why? Is it because,
since I have devoted myself unreserved-
ly to its influencing, I have never felt
happiness? I have rejected all fancy,
all imagination : I find that all pleasure
resulting to self is thereby completely
annihilated. I am led into this egotism,
that you may be clearly aware of the
nature of reason, as it affects me. I
am sincere : will you comment upon
this ?

Adieu.   A picture of Christ hangs
opposite in my room : it is well done,
and has met my look at the conclusion
of this.   Do not believe but that I am
sincere : but am I not too prolix ?
Yours most sincerely,
PERCY SHELLEY.

LETTER III.

FIELD PLACE.
[*Thursday*] *June* 20, 1811.

MY DEAR MADAM,

Your letter, though dated the 14th, has not reached me until this moment.

"Reason sanctions an aberration from reason." I admit it; or rather, on some subjects, I conceive it to command a dereliction of itself. What I mean by this is an habitual analysis of our own thoughts. It is this habit, acquired by length of solitary labour, never then to be shaken off, which induces gloom; which deprives the being thus affected of any anticipation or retrospection of happiness, and leaves him eagerly in pursuit of virtue,—yet (apparent paradox) pursuing it without the weakest stimulus. It is this, then,

against which I intended to caution
you : this is the tree which it is
dangerous to eat, but which 1 have fed
upon to satiety.

We both look around us.   We find
that we exist.   We find ourselves
reasoning upon the mystery which
involves our being.   We see virtue
and vice ; we see light and darkness.
Each is separate, distinct : the line
which divides them is glaringly per-
ceptible.   Yet how racking it is to
the soul, when enquiring into its own
operations, to find that perfect virtue is
very far from attainable,—to find reason
tainted by feeling, to see the mind,
when analysed, exhibit a picture of
irreconcileable inconsistencies, even
when perhaps, a moment before, it
imagined that it had grasped the fleeting phantom of virtue !   But let us
dismiss the subject.

It is still my opinion, for reasons
before mentioned, that Christianity

strongly militates with virtue. Both yourself and Lyttelton are guilty of a mistake of the term "Christian." A Christian is a follower of the religion which has constantly gone by the name of Christianity, as a Mahometan is of Mahometanism. Each of these professors ceases to belong to the sect which either word means, when they set up a doctrine of their own, irreconcileable with that of either religion except in a few instances in which common and self-evident morality coincides with its tenets. It is then morality, virtue, which they set up as the criterion of their actions, and not the *exclusive* doctrine preached by the founder of any religion. Why, your religion agrees as much with Bramah, Zoroaster, or Mahomet, as with Christ. Virtue is self-evident : consequently I act in unison with its dictates when the doctrines of Christ do not differ from virtue ; *there* I follow *them.*

Surely you *then* follow virtue : or you
equally follow Bramah and Mahomet
as Christ. *Your* Christianity does not
interfere with virtue : and why?
Because it is not Christianity!

Yet you still appear to court the
delusion. How is this? Do I know
you as well as I know myself? Then
it is that this religion promises a future
state, which otherwise were a matter at
least of doubt. Let us consider. A
false view of any subject, when a true
one were attainable, were best avoided,
inasmuch as truth and falsehood are in
themselves good and bad. All that natural reason enables us to discover is that
we now are ; that there was a time when
we were not ; that the moment, even,
when we are now reasoning is a point before and after which is eternity. Shall
we sink into the nothing from whence we
have arisen ? But could we have arisen
from nothing ? We put an acorn into the
ground. In process of time it modifies

the particles of earth, air and water
by infinitesimal division, so as to produce an oak. That power which makes
it to be this oak we may call its
vegetative principle, symbolizing with
the animal principle, or soul of animated
existence.

An hundred years pass. The oak
moulders in putrefaction : it ceases to
be what it is : its soul is gone. Is then
soul annihilable? Yet one of the properties of animal soul is consciousness
of identity. If this is destroyed, in
consequence the soul (whose essence
this is) must perish. But, as I conceive
(and as is certainly capable of demonstration) that nothing can be annihilated,
but that everything appertaining to
nature, consisting of constituent parts
infinitely divisible, is in a continual
change, then do I suppose—and I think
I have a right to draw this inference—
that neither will soul perish ; that, in a
future existence, it will lose all conscious-

ness of having formerly lived elsewhere,
—will begin life anew, possibly under
a shape of which we have no idea.—But
we have no right to make hypotheses.
This is not one : at least I flatter myself
that I have kept clear of supposition.

What think you of the bubbling
brooks and mossy banks at Carlton
House,—the *allées vertes*, &c.?   It is
said that this entertainment will cost
£120,000. Nor will it be the last
bauble which the nation must buy to
amuse this overgrown bantling of
Regency. How admirably this grow-
ing spirit of ludicrous magnificence
tallies with the disgusting splendours of
the stage of the Roman Empire which
preceded its destruction ! Yet here
are a people advanced in intellectual
improvement wilfully rushing to a
revolution, the natural death of all
great commercial empires, which must
plunge them in the barbarism from
which they are slowly arising.

DON RODERICK is not yet come out : when it is, you shall see it.—Adieu.

Yours most sincerely,

PERCY SHELLEY.

LETTER IV.

My Dear Madam,

Do not speak any more of my time thrown away, or you will compel me, in my own defence, to say things which, although they could not share in the nature, would participate in the appearance, of compliment.

What you say of the fallen state of Man I will remark upon. Man is fallen. How is he fallen? You see a thing imperfect and diminutive; but you cannot infer that it had degenerated to this state, without first proving that it had anteriorly existed in a perfect state. Apply this rule, the accuracy of which is unquestionable, to Man. Look at history, even the earliest. What does it tell you of Man? An ancient tradition recorded in the Bible (upon the truth or falsehood of which this depends) tells you that Man once existed in a superior state. But how are you to believe this? how, in short, is this to be urged as a proof of the truth of the Scriptures, which itself depends upon the previously demonstrated truth or fallacy of *them*?

You look around, you say; and see in everything a wonderful harmony conspicuous. How know you this? Might not some animal, the victim of man's capricious tyranny, itself possibly the capricious tyrant of another, reason thus? "How wretched, how peculiarly wretched, is our state! In man all is harmony. Their buildings arise in method, their society is united by bonds of indissolubility. All nature, but that of *horses*, is harmonical; and *he* is born to misery only because he is a horse." Yet this reasoning is yours. Surely this applies to all nature : surely this may be called harmony. But then it is the harmony of irregular confusion, which equalizes everything by being itself unequal, wherever it acts.

This brings me again to the point which I aim at—the eternal existence of Intellect. You have read Locke. You are convinced that there are no innate ideas, and that you do not always think when asleep. Yet, let me enquire : in these moments of intellectual suspension do you suppose that the soul is annihilated? You cannot suppose it, knowing the infallibility of the rule—" From nothing, nothing can come : to nothing, nothing can return ; " as, by this rule, it *could* not be annihilated, or, if annihilated, could not be capable of resuscitation. This brings me to the point. Those around the lifeless corpse are perfectly aware that *it* thinks not : at least, they are aware that, when scattered through all the changes which matter undergoes, it

cannot then think. You have witnessed
one suspension of intellect in dreamless
sleep : you witness another in death.
From the first, you well know that you
cannot infer diminution of intellectual
force. How contrary then to all
analogy to infer annihilation from
death, which you cannot prove suspends
for a moment the force of mind.—This
is not hypothesis, this is not assumption :
at least, I am not aware of the admis-
sion of either. Willingly would I
exclude both—would influence *you* to
their total exclusion.

Yet examine this argument with
your reason : tell me the result.

You wish to " pass among those who,
like you, have deceived themselves."
I defy you to produce to me one who
like you has deceived herself. Deceive
the world like yourself, and I will no
longer object to the immoral influence
of Christianity : in short, let the world
be Christians, *like you.* *Let* them not

be Christians, and they *would* not be Christians.

Atheism appears a terrific monster at a distance. Dare to examine it, look at its companions,—it loses half its terrors. In short, treat the word Atheism as you have done that of Christianity : it is not then much. I do not place your wish for justification to prejudice, but to the highest, the noblest, of motives. You have named your God. The worship of *that* God is clear, self-evident, perspicuous : it alone is unceremonious, it alone refuses to contradict natural analogies, can be the subject of no disputes, the countenancer of no misconceptions.

Since we conversed on the subject, I have seen no reason to change my political opinions. In theology,— enquiries into our intellect, its eternity or perishability,—I advance with caution and circumspection. I pursue it in the privacy of retired thought, or the interchange of friendship. But in politics—here I am enthusiastic. I have reasoned; and my reason has brought me, on this subject, to the end of my enquiries. I am no aristocrat, nor any "*crat*" at all; but vehemently long for the time when man may dare to live in accordance with Nature and Reason,— in consequence, with Virtue: to which I firmly believe that Religion, its establishment,—Polity, and *its* establishments,—are the formidable, though destructible, barriers.

We heard from the Captain the other day: I am happy to find that my aunt is recovering.

On Monday I shall be in London on my way to Wales, where I purpose to spend the summer. My excursion will be on foot, for the purpose of better remarking the manners and dispositions of the peasantry. I shall call on you in London, and write to you from the resting-places of my movements.

Your sincere friend,

PERCY SHELLEY.

LETTER V.

Cwm Elan, Rhayader,
Radnorshire.
Thursday [*July* 25, 1811.]

My dear Madam,

Be assured that, as long as you are what you are, as long as I am what I am—which is likely to continue until our *transmigration*—you will always occupy a most exalted place in my warmest esteem. I am no courtier, aristocrat, or loyalist : therefore you may believe that your correspondence would be resigned with the pain of having lost a most valuable thing, when I tell you so.

I am truly sorry to hear that my aunt has not recovered : I shall write to the Captain to-day.

You say that Equality is unattainable : so, will I observe, is Perfection. Yet

they both symbolize in their nature :
they both demand that an unremitting
tendency towards themselves should
be made : and, the nearer society
approaches towards this point, the
happier will it be. No one has yet
been found resolute enough in dog-
matizing to deny that Nature made
man equal : that society has destroyed
this equality is a truth not more in-
controvertible. It is found that the
vilest cottager is often happier than the
proud lord of his manorial rights. Is
it fit that the most frightful passions
of human nature should be let loose,
by an unnatural compact of society,
upon this unhappy aristocrat ? Is he
not to be pitied when, by an hereditary
possession of a fortune which, if divided,
would have very different effects, he is,
as it were, predestined to dissipation,
ennui, self-reproach, and (to crown the
climax) a deathbed of despairing inutility ? It is often found that the

peasant's life is embittered by the
commission of crime.—(Yet can we
call it crime? Certainly, when we
compare the seizure of a few shillings
from the purse of a Nobleman, to preserve a beloved family from starving, to
the destruction which the unrestrained
propensities of this Nobleman scatter
around him, we may almost call it
virtue).—To what cause are we to
refer this? The noble has too much :
therefore he is wretched and wicked.
The peasant has too little. Are not
then the consequences the same from
causes which nothing but Equality can
annihilate? And, although you may
consider equality as impossible, yet,
admitting this, a strenuous tendency
towards it appears recommended by the
consequent diminution of wickedness
and misery which my system holds
out. Is this to be denied? Ridicule perfection as impossible. Do more : prove
it by arguments which are irresistible.

Let the defender of perfection acknow-
ledge 'their cogency. Still, a strenuous
tendency towards this principle, however unattainable, cannot be considered
as wrong.

You are willing to dismiss for the
present the subject of Religion. As
to its influence on individuals, we will.
But it is so intimately connected with
politics, and augments in so vivid a
degree the evils resulting from the
system before us, that I will make a
few remarks on it. Shall I sum up the
evidence ? It is needless. The per-
secutions against the Christians under
the Greek Empire, their energetic
retaliations and burning each other, the
excommunications bandied between
the Popes of Rome and the Patriarchs
of Constantinople, their influence upon politics (war, assassination, the
Sicilian Vespers, the Massacre of St.
Bartholomew, Lord G. Gordon's mob,
and the state of religious things at

present), can amply substantiate my assertions.

And Liberty !—Poor Liberty ! even the religionists who cry so much for thee use thy name but as a mask, that they alone may seize the torch, and show their gratitude by burning their deliverer.

I should doubt the existence of a God who, if he cannot command our reverence by love, surely can have no demand upon it, from Virtue, on the score of terror. It is this empire of terror which is established by Religion. Monarchy is its prototype : Aristocracy may be regarded as symbolizing with its very essence. They are mixed : one can now scarce be distinguished from the other ; and equality in politics, like perfection in morality, appears now far removed from even the visionary anticipations of what is called "the wildest theorist." *I*, then, am wilder than the wildest.

I am happy that you like *Kehama*. Is not the chapter where Kailyal despises the leprosy grand? You would like also *Joan of Arc* by Southey.—Whenever I have any new books, I will send them to you.

I will write again soon. I now remain, with the highest esteem,

Yours sincerely,

PERCY SHELLEY.

LETTER VI.

Cwm Elan.
[*Friday*] *July* 26, 1811.

My dear Madam,

I wrote to you yesterday in a great hurry; at least, very much interfered with. I began politics; and although, from the mental discussion which I have given the subject, I do not think my arguments are inconclusive, still they may be obscure.

What I contend for is this. Were I a moral legislator, I would propose to my followers that they should arrive at the perfection of morality. Equality is natural: at least, many evils totally inconsistent with a state which symbolizes with Nature prevail in every system of inequality. I will assume this point. Therefore, even although it be your opinion, or my opinion, that equality is unattainable except by a parcel of peas, or beans, still political virtue is to be estimated in proportion as it approximates to this ideal point of perfection, however unattainable. But what can be worse than the present aristocratical system? Here are, in England, 10,000,000, only 500,000 of whom live in a state of ease: the rest earn their livelihood with toil and care. If therefore these 500,000 aristocrats, who possess resources of various degrees of immensity, were to permit these resources to be resolved into their original stock (that is, entirely to destroy it), if each earned his own living (which I do not see is at all incompatible with the height of intellectual refinement), then I affirm that each would be happy and con_ tented—that crime, and the temptation to crime, would scarcely exist.—" But this paradise is all visionary."—Why is it visionary? Have you tried? The first inventor of a plough doubtless was looked upon as a mad innovator: he who altered it from its original absurd form doubtless had to contend with great prejudices in its disfavour. But is it not worth while that (although it may not be *certain*) the remaining 9,500,000 victims to its infringement [should] make some exertions in favour of a system evidently founded on the first principles of natural justice? If two children were placed together in a desert island, and they found some scarce fruit, would not justice dictate an equal division? If this number is multiplied to any extent of which number is capable,—if these children are men, families,—is not justice capable of the same extension and multiplication? Is it not the same? Are not its decrees invariable? and, for the sake of his earth-formed schemes, has the politician a right to infringe upon that which itself constitutes all right and wrong? Surely not.

I know *why* you differ from me on this point. It is because you suspect yourself of partiality for the cause with which you agree. I must say, my friend and fellow-traveller in the path of truth, that this is wrong. You are unworthy of the suspicion with which you regard yourself.

I am now with people who, strange to say, never *think :* I have, however, much more of my own society than of theirs. Nature is here marked with the most impressive characters of lordliness and grandeur. Once I was tremulously alive to tones and scenes : the habit of analysing feelings, I fear, does not agree with this. It is spontaneous; and, when it becomes subject to consideration, ceases to exist. But you do right to indulge feeling, where it does not militate with reason : I wish I could too.

This valley is covered with trees : so are partly the mountains that surround it. Rocks, piled on each other to an immense height, and clouds intersecting them,—in other places, waterfalls midst the umbrage of a thousand shadowy trees,—form the principal features of the scenery. I am not wholly uninfluenced by its magic in my lonely walks. But I long for a thunderstorm.

Adieu : let me soon hear from you.

Your most sincere friend,

P. B. SHELLEY.

LETTER VII.

LONDON.

[*Saturday*] *Aug.* 10, 1811.

MY DEAR MADAM,

I understand that there is a letter for me at Cwm Elan. I have not received it. Particular business has occasioned my sudden return. I shall be at Field Place to-morrow, and shall possibly see you before September.

My engagements have hindered much devotion of time to a consideration of the subject of our discussion. I here see palaces the thirtieth part of which would bless with every requisite of habitation, their pampered owners; theatres converted from schools of morality into places for the inculcation of abandonment of every moral principle; whilst the haughty aristocrat and the commercial monopolist unite in sanctioning by example the depravities to which the importations of the latter give rise.

All monopolies are bad. I do not, however, when condemning commercial aggrandizement, think it in the least necessary to panegyrize hereditary accumulation. Both are flagrant encroachments on liberty : neither can be used as an antidote for the poison of the other. We will suppose even the best aristocrat. Yet look at our noblemen : take the Court Calendar : hear even what the world, who judges favourably of grandeur, narrates concerning their actions. The very encomia which it confers are insults to reason. Take the best aristocrat. He monopolizes a large house, gold dishes, glittering dresses : his very servants are decked in magnificence. How does one monopoly differ from another,—that of the mean Duke from that of the mean pacer between the pillars of the Exchange ?

Having once established the position that a state of equality, if attainable, were preferable to any other, I think that the unavoidable inference must induce us to confess the irrationality of Aristocracy. Intellectual inequality could never be obviated until moral perfection be attained : then all distinctions would be levelled.

Adieu.

LETTER VIII.

[*Monday,*] *August* 19*th*, [1811.]

My dear Madam,

Your letter yesterday disappointed me; not because it set me right in one of those trivial sacrifices to custom which I am wont, through their real unimportance, to overlook, but because, in place of liberal ideas which have ever marked those characters of your mind which I have had an opportunity of observing, I noticed that you said : "though *you* should have disregarded the real difference that exists between us." You remind me thus of a misfortune which I could never have obviated : not that the sturdiest aristocrat could suppose that a real difference sub- sisted between me, who am sprung from a race of rich men, and you, whom talents and virtue have lifted from the obscurity of poverty. If there is any difference, surely the balance of real distinction would fall on your side. You remind me of what I hate, despise, and shudder at, what willingly I would not : and the part which I can emancipate myself from, in this detestable coil of primæval prejudice, that *will* I free myself from. Have I not forsworn all this ? Am I not a worshipper of Equality? It was the custom, even with the Jews, never to insult the Gods of other nations : why then do you put a sarcasm so galling upon the object of my adoration ?

Let us consider. In a former letter you say that "Nature has decidedly distinguished degrees among a degenerate race." Admit for a moment that the composition of soul varies in every recipient, still Nature must have been blind to give a kingdom to a fool, a dukedom to a sensualist, an empire to a tyrant. If she *thus* distinguishes degrees, how does the wildest anarchy differ from Nature's law ? or rather, how are they not, by this account, synonymous ?—Again : Soul may be proved to be, not that which changes its first principles in every new recipient, but an elementary essence, an essence of first principles which bears the mark of casual or of intended impressions. For instance : the non-existence of innate ideas is proved by Locke ; he challenges any one to find an idea which *is* innate. This is conclusive. If no ideas are innate, then all ideas must take their origin subsequent to the transfusion of the soul. In consequence of this indisputable truth, intellect varies but in the impressions with which casuality or inattention has marked it. When is now *Nature*, distinguishing degrees ? or rather do you not see that Art has assumed that office, even in the gifts of the mind ?

I see the *impropriety* of dining with you—even of calling upon you. I shall not willingly, however, give up the friendship and correspondence of one whom, however superior to me, my arrogance calls an equal.

Adieu.

Yours most sincerely,

PERCY S.

Excuse the haste in which I write this.

LETTER IX.

.

YORK. MISS DANCER'S, CONEY STREET.
[*Tuesday*, 8 *October*, 1811.]

MY DEAR FRIEND,

May I still call you so? or have
I forfeited, by the equivocality of my
conduct, the esteem of the wise and
virtuous? have I disgraced the professions of that virtue which has been
the idol of my love, whose votaries
have been the brothers and sisters or
my soul?

When last I saw you, 1 was about to
enter into the profession of physic. 1
told you so. I represented my views
as unembarrassed; myself at liberty to
experiment upon morality, uninfluenced
by the possibility of giving pain to
others. You will know that my
relational connexions were such as

could have no hold but that of con-
sanguinity: how weak this is may be
referred to the bare feeling to explain.
I saw you.   In one short week, how
changed were all my prospects! How
are we the slaves of circumstances!
how bitterly I curse their bondage!
Yet this was unavoidable.

You will enquire how I, an Atheist,
chose to subject myself to the ceremony
of marriage,—how my conscience could
consent to it.   This is all I am now
anxious of elucidating.   Why I united
myself thus to a female, as it is not in
itself immoral, can make no part in
diminution of my rectitude: *this*, if
misconceived, may.

I am indifferent to reputation : all are
not.   Reputation, and its consequent
advantages, are rights to which every
individual may lay claim, unless he has
justly forfeited them by an immoral
action.   Political rights also, which
justly appertain equally to each, ought

only to be forfeited by immorality. Yet both of these must be dispensed with, if two people live together without having undergone the ceremony of marriage. How unjust this is ! Certainly it is not inconsistent with morality to evade these evils. How useless to attempt, by singular examples, to renovate the face of society, until reasoning has made so comprehensive a change as to emancipate the experimentalist from the resulting evils, and the prejudice with which his opinion (which ought to have weight, for the sake of virtue) would be heard by the immense majority !—These are my reasons.

Will you write to me? Shall we proceed in our discussions of Nature and Morality? Nay more: will you be my friend, may I be yours? The shadow of worldly impropriety is effaced by *my* situation. Our strictest intercourse would excite none of those disgusting remarks with which *females* of the present day think right to load the friendships of opposite sexes. Nothing would be transgressed by your even living with us. Could you not pay me a visit? My dear friend Hogg, that noble being, is with me, and will be always: but my wife will abstract from our intercourse the shadow of impropriety. How happy should I be to see you! There is no need to tell you this; and my happiness is not so great that it becomes a friend to be sparing in that society which constitutes its only charm.

I will close this letter. I have enough to say, but will wait for your answer until I write again.

Your great friend,
P. B. SHELLEY.

LETTER X.

York,
[*Wednesday*, 16] *October*, 1811.

I write to-day, because not to
answer such a letter as yours instantly,
eagerly—I will add, gratefully—were
impossible. But I shall be at Cuckfield
on Friday night. My dearest friend
(for I will call you so), you, who understand my motives to action, which, I
flatter myself, unisionize with your own,
—you, who can contemn the world's
prejudices, whose views are mine,—I
will dare to say I *love:* nor do I risk
the possibility of that degrading and
contemptible interpretation of this
sacred word, nor do I risk the supposition that the lump of organized
matter which enshrines thy soul excites
the love which that soul alone dare

claim. Henceforth will I be yours—
yours with truth, sincerity, and unreserve.
Not a thought shall arise which shall
not seek its responsion in your bosom ;
not a motive of action shall be un-
enwafted by your cooler reason : and, by
so doing, do I not choose a criterion
more infallible than my own consciousness of right and wrong (though this
may not be required)? for what conflict
of a frank mind is more terrible than the
balance between two opposing impart-
ances of morality? This is surely the
only wretchedness which a mind who
only acknowledges virtue its master can
feel.

I leave York to-night for Cuckfield,
where I shall arrive on Friday. That
mistaken man, my father, has refused
us money, and commanded that our
names should never be mentioned. I
had thought that this blind resentment
had long been banished to the regions
of Dullness, comedies and farces ; or

was used merely to augment the difficulties, and consequently the attachment, of the hero and heroine of a modern novel. I have written frequently to this thoughtless man, and am now determined to visit him, in order to try the force of truth ; though I must confess I consider it merely as hyperbolical as "music rending the knotted oak." Some philosophers have ascribed indefiniteness to the powers of intellect ; but I question whether it ever would make an ink-stand capable of free agency. Is this too severe ? But, you know, I, like the God of the Jews, set myself up as no respecter of persons ; and relationship is considered by me as bearing that relation to reason which a band of straw does to fire. I love *you* more than any relation ; I profess you are the sister of my soul, its dearest sister; and I think the component parts of that soul must undergo complete dissolution before its sympathies can perish.

Some philosophers have taken a world of pains to persuade us that congeniality is but romance. Certainly, reason can never either account for, or prove the truth of, feeling. I have considered it in every possible light; and reason tells me that death is the boundary of the life of man : yet I feel, I believe, the direct contrary. The senses are the only inlets of knowledge, and there is an inward sense that has persuaded me of this.

How I digress! how does one reasoning lead to another, involving a chain of endless considerations! Certainly, everything is connected. Both in the moral and physical world there is a train of events; and (though not likely) it is impossible to deny that the turn which my mind has taken originated from the conquest of England by William of Normandy.

By the bye, I have something to talk to you of—Money. I covet it.— "What, you? you a miser! you desire gold! you a slave to the most contemptible of ambitions!"—No, I am not; but I still desire money, and I desire it because I think I know the use of it. It commands labour, it gives leisure; and to give leisure to those who will employ it in the forwarding of truth is the noblest present an individual can make to the whole. I will open to you my views. On my coming to the estate which, worldly considered, is mine, but which actually I have not more, perhaps not so great a right to, as you,—justice demands that it should be shared between my sisters. Does it, or does it not? Mankind are as much my brethren and sisters as they: *all* ought to share. This cannot be; it must be confined. But thou art a sister of my soul, *he* is its brother: surely these have a right.

Consider this subject, write to me on
it. Divest yourself of individuality:
dare to place self at a distance, which
I know you can: spurn those bugbears,
gratitude, obligation, and modesty.
The world calls these "virtues." They
are well enough for the world. It
wants a chain: it hath forged one for
itself. But with the sister of my soul
I have no obligation: to her I feel no
gratitude: I stand not on etiquette,
alias insincerity. The ideas excited by
these words are varying, frequently unjust, always selfish. Love, in the sense
in which *we* understand it, needs not
these *succedanea.*—Consider the question which I have proposed to you. I
know you are above that pretended
confession of your own imbecility which
the world has nicknamed modesty, and
you must be conscious of your own high
worth. To underrate your powers is an
evil of greater magnitude than the contrary: the former benumbs, whilst the

latter excites to action. My friend
Hogg and myself consider our property
in common: that the day will arrive
when *we* shall do the same is the wish
of my soul, whose consummation I
most eagerly anticipate.

My uncle is a most generous fellow.
Had he not assisted us, we should still
[have] been chained to the filth and
commerce of Edinburgh. Vile as aristocracy is, commerce — purse-proud
ignorance and illiterateness—is more
contemptible.

I still see Religion to be immoral.
When I contemplate these gigantic
piles of superstition—when I consider,
too, the leisure for the exercise of mind
which the labour which erected them
annihilated—I set them down as so
many retardations of the period when
Truth becomes omnipotent. Every
useless ornament—the pillars, the iron
railings, the juttings of wainscot, and
(as Southey says) the cleaning of grates

—are all exertions of bodily labour
which—though trivial, separately considered,—when united, destroy a vast
proportion of this invaluable leisure.
How many things could we do without! How unnecessary are *mahogany*
tables, silver vases, myriads of viands
and liquors, expensive printing,—that,
worst of all. Look even [around some]
little habitation,—the dirtiest cottage,
which [exhibits] myriads of instances
where ornament is sacrificed [? pre-
ferred] to cleanliness or leisure.

Whither do I wander? Certainly, I
wish to prove, by my own proper
prowess, that the chain which I spoke
of is real.

The letter at Field Place has been
opened and read, exposed to all the
remarks of impertinence : not that they
understood it.

Henceforth I shall have no secrets
from you; and indeed I have much
then to tell you—wonderful changes !

Direct to me at the Captain's until you
hear again : but I only stay two days
in Sussex,—but I shall see you.

Sister of my soul, adieu.

With, I hope, eternal love,

Your

PERCY SHELLEY.

LETTER XI.

CUCKFIELD.

[*Saturday,* 19 *October,* 1811.?]

I do not know that I shall have time to see you, my dear friend, whilst in Sussex. On Monday or Tuesday I *must* return. The intervening periods will be employed in the hateful task of combating prejudice and mistake. Yet our souls can meet, for these become embodied on paper: all else is even emptier than the breath of fame.

I omitted mentioning something in my last: 'tis of your visiting us. You say that *at some remote period*, &c. What is this remote period? when will it arrive? The term is indefinite, and friendship cannot be satisfied with this. I do not mean to-day, to-morrow, or this week; but the time approaches when you need not attend the business of the school : *then* you have your own choice to make of the place of your intermediate residence. If that choice were in favour of me !

I shall come to live in this county. My friend Hogg, Harriet, my new sister, . . . could but be added to these the sister of my soul ! *That* I cannot hope : but still she may visit us.

I have been convinced of the eventual omnipotence of mind over matter. Adequacy of motive is sufficient to anything : and *my* Golden Age is when the present potence will become omnipotence. This will be the millennium of Christians, when "the lion shall lie down with the lamb ": though neither will it be accomplished to complete a prophecy, nor by the intervention of a miracle. This has been the favourite idea of all religions, the thesis on which the impassioned and benevolent have delighted to dwell. Will it not be the task of human reason, human powers,—

whose progression in improvement has been so great since the remotest tradition, tracing general history to the point where now we stand? The series is infinite—can never end!

Now you will laugh at what I am about to tell you. Whence think [you] this reasoning has arisen? Just [conceive] its possible origin! Never [could] you have [conceived] that three days on the outside of a coach caused it. [Yet] so it is. I am now at Cuckfield; I arrived this morning; and, though three nights without sleep, I feel now neither sleepy nor fatigued. *This* is adequacy of motive. During my journey I had the proposed end in view of accumulating money to myself for the motives which I stated in my last letter.

I know I have something more to tell you—I forget what. The Captain is talking.

I must settle my plan of attack to-morrow.

Adieu, my dear friend.

Your

PERCY S.

I am happy to hear what I have just heard. You are to come to dine here, and bring Emma, on Monday 21st, in the coach.

LETTER XII.

MR. STRICKLAND'S, BLAKE ST., YORK.

[*Saturday*, 26 *October*, 1811.?]

It is no "generosity": it is justice—
bare, simple justice. Oh, to what a
state must poor human nature have
arrived when simply to do our duty
merits praise! Let us delight in the
anticipation (though it may not be *our*
lot to breathe that air of paradise) that
the time will arrive when all that now
is called generosity will be simply,
barely duty. But you *shall not* refuse
it. Private feelings must not be grati-
fied at the expense of public benefit by
your refusal: deeply would the latter
suffer. I know you speak from conviction; nor, except from conviction,
should I allow you to act as far as concerns me. It is impossible that you
should do otherwise. Yet I hope to

produce that conviction. You cannot be convinced—quite convinced. It is impossible that any one should thoroughly know themselves, particularly in an instance like this, where self-deceit is so likely to creep in from the contagious sophistications of society, and, assuming the garb of virtue, represent itself to you as its substance. I know you to be superior to that mock-modesty of self-depreciation : this therefore has no weight. See yourself, then, as you are. I esteem you more than I esteem myself. Am I not right therefore in giving you at least equal opportunities of conferring on mankind the benefits of that which has excited this esteem ? You may *then* share your possessions with that friend whom I ardently long to know and to love, but who must receive the tribute of gratitude from you,—though, if she has made you what you are, what claims may not just retribution make upon me in her behalf?

I have thus said what I think, at least two years before I can accomplish the projects which I have to execute. "It is the mere prodigality of promise," would the slave of others' opinion exclaim, "never to be executed: two months will dissipate the sickly ravings; it demands two years of uniform opinion." Let them thus rave,—'tis their element! But, whilst the sister of my soul, the friend of my heart, knows its unchangeableness, how futile are these gnat-bites! But it is necessary that the world should not know this: to preserve in some measure the good opinion of Prejudice is necessary to its destruction. This must be the most secret of communications: thine are most sacredly secret to me. But the time you lose in thus acquiring money for the noblest of human purposes would be saved by your acceptance of my offer. There are two years, however, to argue this subject in. We

have now begun : I am convinced that
I shall conquer.

When may I see the woman who
indeed deserves my love, if she was thy
instructress ? Let not the period be
very distant. I already reverence her
as a mother. How useful are such
characters ! how they propagate intellect, and add to the list of the virtuous
and free ! Every error conquered, every
mind enlightened, is so much added to
the progression of human perfectibility.
Sure, such as you, then, ought to
possess the amplest leisure for a task to
the completion of which each of those
excellencies which excite my love for
you is so adapted. Believe that I do
not flatter ; suspect me not of rash
judgment. My judgment of you has
been unimpassioned, though *now* un-
impassionateness is over, and I *could*
not believe you other than the being I
have hitherto considered as enshrined
in the identity of Elizabeth Hitchener.

I hesitate not a moment to write to you : rare though it be in this existence, communion with you can unite mental benefit with *pure* gratification. I will explain, however, the circumstances which caused my marriage : these must certainly have caused much conjecture in your mind.

Some time ago, when my sister was at Mrs. Fenning's school, she contracted an intimacy with Harriet. At that period I attentively watched over my sister, designing, if possible, to add her to the list of the good, the disinterested, the free. I desired therefore to investigate Harriet's character : for which purpose I called on her, requested to correspond with her, designing that *her* advancement should keep pace with, and possibly accelerate, that of my sister. Her ready and frank acceptance of my proposal pleased me ; and, though with ideas the remotest to those which have led to this conclusion of our intimacy, [I] continued to correspond with her for some time. The frequency of her letters became greater during my stay in Wales. I answered them : they became interesting. They contained complaints of the irrational conduct of her relations, and the misery of living where she could *love* no one. Suicide was with her a favourite theme, her total uselessness was urged in its defence. This I admitted, supposing she could prove her inutility, [and that she] was powerless. Her letters became more and more [gloomy]. At length one assumed a tone of such despair as induced me to quit Wales precipitately. I arrived in London. I was shocked at observing the alteration of her looks. Little did I divine its cause : she had become violently attached to me, and feared that I should not return her attachment. Prejudice made the confession painful. It was impossible to avoid being much affected I promised

to unite my fate with hers. I stayed in
London several days, during which she
recovered her spirits. I had promised at
her bidding to come again to London.
They endeavoured to compel her to
return to a school where malice and
pride embittered every hour : she wrote
to me. I came to London. I proposed marriage, for the reasons which
I have given you, and she complied.—
Blame me if thou wilt, dearest friend,
for *still* thou art dearest to me : yet pity
even this error, if thou blamest me.
If Harriet be not, at sixteen, all that
you are at a more advanced age, assist
me to mould a really noble soul into
all that can make its nobleness useful
and lovely. Lovely it is now, or I am
the weakest slave of error.

Adieu to this subject until I hear
again from you. Write soon, in pity
to my suspense.

We did not call on Whitton as we
passed. We find he means absolutely

nothing : he talks of disrespect, duty, &c.

I observed that you were much shocked at my mother's depravity. I have heard some reasons (and as mere reasons they are satisfactory) that there is no such thing as moral depravity. But it does not prove the non-existence of a thing that it is not discoverable by reason : *feeling* here affords us sufficient proof. I pity those who have not this demonstration, though I can scarce believe that such exist.

Those who *really feel* the being of a God, have the best right to believe it. They may, indeed, pity those who do not ; they may pity me : but, until I feel it, I must be content with the sub stitute, Reason.

Here is a letter !—well, answer some of it,—though I allow 'tis terribly long.

Southey has published something new —*The Bridal of Fernandez :* have you seen it? Have you read *St. Leon* or *Caleb Williams?*

Adieu, dear friend. Believe me
Ever yours sincerely,
PERCY B. SHELLEY.

Have you heard anything of Captain P[ilford's] proceedings at F[ield] P[lace]?—I have more to say, but no more room, so adieu.

LETTER XIII.

[KESWICK,
Friday, 8 *November*, 1811. ?]

My friend will be surprised to hear
of me from Keswick in Cumberland :
more so will [she] be astonished at the
occasion.   It is a thing that makes my
blood run cold to think of.   I almost
lose my confidence in the power of
truth, its unalterableness.   Human nature appears so depraved.   Even those
in whom we place unlimited confidence,
between whom and yourself suspicion
never came, appear depraved as the
rest.   High powers appear but to present opportunities for occasioning superior misery.   Can it be thus always ?

You know how I have described
Hogg,—my enthusiasm in his defence,
my love for him.   You know I have
considered him but little below perfec-

tion. I have spoken to you of him—
have described him not with the exag-
gerations but with the truth of friendship. I have resolved, because I am
your friend, to make you the deposi-
tary of a secret : it is to me a most
terrible one.

Hogg is a mistaken man—vilely,
dreadfully mistaken. But you shall
hear; then judge of the extent of the
evil which I deplore. That he whom
my fond expectations had pictured the
champion of virtue, the enemy of prejudice, should himself become the
meanest slave of the most contemptible
of prejudices, is indeed dreadful. But
listen. How fast you read this! I
fancy I behold you !

You know I came to Sussex to settle
my affairs, and left Harriet at York
under the protection of Hogg. You
know the implicit faith I had in him,
the unalterableness of my attachment,
the exalted thoughts I entertained of

his excellence. Can you then conceive that he would have attempted to *seduce my wife?* that he should have chosen the very time for this attempt when I most confided in him, when least I doubted him? Yet when did I *ever* doubt him? Yet, my friend, this is the case. And such an attempt! You may conceive his sophistry; you may conceive the energy of vice, for energy is inseparable from high powers: but never could you conceive, never having experienced it, that resistless and pathetic eloquence of his, never the illumination of that countenance, on which I have sometimes gazed till I fancied the world could be reformed by gazing too! You—you have never seen him, never heard him; or Harriet would have stood first in your regards as the heroic, or the unfeeling, who could have done other than as he directed. The *latter* she is not.

Conjecture, conceive, friend, how I

love you! how firm my reliance is on
your principles, how impossible to be
shaken is my faith in your nobleness!
Then, then imagine what I have felt at
losing by so terrible a reverse, a friend
like you—lost too not only to me but
to the world! Virtue has lost one of
its defenders, Vice has gained a prose-
lyte. The thought makes me shudder!
But must it be thus? Cannot I pre-
vent it? cannot I reason with him?
Is he dead, cold, gone, annihilated?
None, none of these! therefore *not*
irretrievable—*not* fallen like Lucifer,
never to rise again!

Before I quitted York, I spoke to
him. Our conversation was long. He
was silent, pale, over-whelmed. The
suddenness of the disclosure—and oh
I hope its heinousness—had affected
him. I told him that I pardoned him
—freely, fully, completely pardoned;
that not the least anger against him
possessed me. His vices, and not

himself, were the objects of my horror and my hatred. I told him I yet ardently panted for his real welfare; but that ill-success in crime and misery appeared to me an earnest of its opposite in benevolence. I engaged him to promise to write to me. You can conjecture that my letters to him will be neither infrequent nor short.

I have little time to-day, but I pay this short tribute to friendship. Never, dearest friend, may you experience a disappointment so keen as mine ! Write. I am at Mr. D. Crosthwaite's, Townhead, Keswick, Cumberland. The scenery is awfully grand : it even affects me in such a time as this. Adieu : write to me. I am in need of your sympathy.

Harriet and her sister liked this part of the country; and *I* was, at the moment of our sudden departure, indifferent to all places.

A letter, I suppose, is waiting for me

at York. H. will forward them. Adieu,
my almost only friend.

Yours eternally, sincerely,

PERCY B. SHELLEY.

LETTER XIV.

[Chesnut Cottage, Keswick.
Tuesday, 11 *November,* 1811].

Your letter of the 1st hath this moment reached me. I answer it according to our agreement, which shall be inviolable.

Truly did you say that, at our arising in the morning, Nature assumes a different aspect. Who could have conjectured the circumstances of my last letter? Friend of my soul, this is terrible, dismaying: it makes one's heart sink, it withers vital energy. Had a common man done so, 'twould have been but a common event, but a common mistake. *Now,* if for a moment the soul forgets (as at times it will) that it must enshrine the body for others, how beautiful does death

appear, what a release from the crimes
and miseries of mortality ! To be con-
demned to feed on the garbage of
grinding misery, that hungry hyæna,
mortal life !—But no ! I will not, I do
not, repine. Dear being, I am thine
again : thy happiness shall again
predominate over this fleeting tribute
to self-interest. Yet who would not
feel now ? Oh 'twere as reckless a
task to endeavour to annihilate perception while sense existed, as to blunt
the sixth sense to such impressions as
these !—Forgive me, dearest friend !
I pour out my whole soul to you. I
write by fleeting intervals : my pen
runs away with my senses. The impassionateness of my sensations grows
upon me.

Your letter, too, has much affected me. Never, with my consent,
shall that intercourse cease which has
been the day-dawn of my existence,
the sun which has shed warmth on the

cold drear length of the anticipated prospect of life. Prejudice might demand this sacrifice, but she is an idol to whom *we* bow not. The world might demand it ; its opinion might require : but the cloud which fleets over yon mountain were as important to our happiness, to our usefulness. This must *never* be, never whilst this existence continues; and, when Time has enrolled us in the list of the departed, surely this one friendship will survive to bear our identity to heaven.

What is love, or friendship? Is it something material—a ball, an apple, a plaything—which must be taken from one to be given to another? Is it capable of no extension, no communication? Lord Kaimes defines love to be a particularization of the general passion. But this is the love of sensation, of sentiment—the absurdest of absurd vanities: it is the love of pleasure, not the love of happiness. The one is a love which is self-centred, self-devoted, self-interested: it desires its own interest: it is the parent of jealousy. Its object is the plaything which it desires to monopolize. Selfishness, monopoly, is its very soul; and to communicate to others part of this love were to destroy its essence, to annihilate this chain of straw. But love, the love which *we* worship,— virtue, heaven, disinterestedness—in a word, Friendship,—which has as much to do with the senses as with yonder mountains; that which seeks the good of all,—the good of its object first, not because that object is a minister to its pleasures, not merely because it even contributes to its happiness, but because it is really worthy, because it has powers, sensibilities, is capable of abstracting self, and loving virtue for virtue's own loveliness,—desiring the happiness of others

not from the obligation of fearing hell
or desiring heaven ; but for pure, simple,
unsophisticated virtue.

You will soon hear again. Adieu,
my dearest friend. Continue to believe that when I am insensible to
your excellence, I shall cease to exist.

Yours most sincerely,

inviolably, eternally,

PERCY S.

I have filled my sheet before I
was aware of it. I told Harriet of your
scruples, for which there is not the
slightest foundation. You have mistaken her character, if you consider
her a slave to this meanest of mean
jealousies. She desires to add something : I have scarcely room for her.

Southey lives at Keswick. I
have been contemplating the outside
of his house. More of him hereafter.

Write : I need not tell you, write.
I am in need of your letters.

Harriet desires her love to you and

begs you will not entertain so unfavourable an opinion of her. She desires me to say that she longs to see you,—to welcome you to our habitation, wherever we are, as my best friend and sister.

Direct me at Chesnut Cottage, Mr. Dayer's, Keswick, Cumberland.

LETTER XV.

Keswick, Chesnut Hill, Cumberland.
[*Thursday*, 14 *November*, 1811].

My dearest Friend,

Probably my letters have not left Keswick sufficiently long for your answer, I have more to tell you, however, which relates to this late terrible affair.

The day we left him, he wrote several letters to me,—the first evidently in the frenzy of his disappointment (for I had not told him the *time* of our departure). "I *will* have Harriet's forgiveness, or blow my brains out at her feet." The others, being written in moments of tranquillity, appeased immediate alarm on that score. You are already surprised, shocked : I can conceive it. Oh, it is terrible ! this stroke

has almost withered my being ! Were it
not for that dear friend whose happiness I so much prize, which at some
future period I may perhaps constitute,—did I not live for an end, an
aim, sanctified, hallowed, — I *might*
have slept in peace. Yet no—not
quite that : I might have been a colo-
nist of Bedlam.

Stay : I promised to relate the circumstances. I will proceed histori-
cally.

I had observed that Harriet's beha-
viour to my friend had been greatly
altered : I saw she regarded him with
prejudice and hatred. I saw it with
great pain, and remarked it to her.
Her dark hints of his unworthiness
alarmed me, yet alarmed me vaguely ;
for, believe me, this alarm was un-
tainted with the slightest suspicion of
his disloyalty to virtue and friendship.
Conceive my horror when, on pressing
the conversation, the secret of his un-

faithfulness was divulged! I sought
him, and we walked to the fields beyond York. I desired to know fully
the account of this affair. I heard it
from him, and I believe he was sincere.
All I can recollect of that terrible day
was that I pardoned him—freely, fully
pardoned him; that I would still be a
friend to him, and hoped soon to convince him how lovely virtue was; that
his crime, not himself, was the object
of my detestation; that I value a
human being, not for what it has been,
but for what it is; that I hoped the
time would come when he would regard this horrible error with as much
disgust as I did. He said little: he
was pale, terror-struck, remorseful.

This character is *not* his own: it sits
ill upon him,—it will not long be his.
His account was this. He came to
Edinburgh. He saw me; he saw
Harriet. He loved her (I use the
word because he used it. You com-

prehend the different ideas it excites under different modes of application). He loved her. This passion, so far from meeting with resistance, was encouraged,—purposely encouraged, from motives which then appeared to him not wrong. On our arrival at York, he avowed it. Harriet forbade other mention ; yet forbore to tell me, hoping she might hear no more of it. On my departure from York to Sussex (when you saw me), he urged the same suit,—urged it with arguments of detestable sophistry. " There is no injury to him who knows it not :—why is it wrong to permit my love, if it does not alienate affection ? " These failed of success. At last, Harriet talked to him much of its immorality : and (though I fear her arguments were such as *could not* be logically superior to his) he confessed to her his conviction of having acted wrong, and, as some expiation, proposed instantly to inform *me* by letter of the whole. This Harriet refused to permit, fearing its effect upon my mind at such a distance : she could not know *when* I should return home. I returned the very next day.

This, as near as I recollect, was the substance of what cool consideration can extract from his account. The circumstances are true : Harriet's account coincides.

I have since written to him—frequently, and at great length. His letters are exculpatory : you shall see them.—Adieu at present to the subject.

No, my dearest friend, I will never cease to write to you. I never can cease to think of you.

Happiness, fleeting creation of circumstances, where art thou? I read your letter with delight; but this delight is even mixed with melancholy. And you ! Tell me that you too are unhappy,—the cup of my misfortunes is then completed to the dregs. Yet

did you not say that we should stimu-
late each other to virtue? Shall
I be the first to fail? No! This
listless torpor of regret will never
do—it never shall possess me. Behold me then reassuming myself, de-
serving your esteem,—you, my second
self!

Harriet has laughed at your sup-
positions. She invites you to our
habitation wherever we are : she does
this sincerely, and bids me send her
love to you.

Eliza, her sister, is with us. She is,
I think, a woman rather superior to
the generality. She is prejudiced ; but
her prejudices I do not consider un-
vanquishable. Indeed, I have already
conquered some of them.

The scenery here is awfully beautiful. Our window commands a view of
two lakes, and the giant mountains
which confine them. But the object most interesting to my feelings is

Southey's habitation. He is now on a journey: when he returns, I shall call on him.

Adieu, dearest friend.

Ever yours, with true devotement and love,

PERCY SHELLEY.

LETTER XVI.

Keswick, Cumberland.

[*Wednesday,* 20 *November,* 1811.]

WRITING is slow, soulless, incommunicative. I long to talk with you. My soul is bursting. Ideas, millions of ideas, are crowding into it: it pants for communion with you.

Your letter, too, has affected me deeply. You must not quite despair of human nature. Our conceptions are scarcely vivid enough to picture the degree of crime, of degradation, which sullies human society: but what words are equal to express their inadequacy to picture its hidden virtue? My friend, my dear only friend, never doubt virtue so long as yourself exists. Be yourself a living proof that human nature is a creation of its own, resolves its own determinations; that on the vividness of these depends the intensity of our characters.

It was a terrible, a soul-appalling fall : but it was not, it could not be, a fall never to rise again. It shall not, if I can retrieve it. He desires to live with us again. His supplications (if his letters are, as mine have been, the language of his soul) have much of ardency, passionateness, and sincerity, in them. But this must not be. I have endeavoured to judge on this subject, if possible, with disinterestedness ; and I think I owe to Harriet's happiness and his reformation that this should not be. Keen as might have been my feelings, I think, if virtue compelled it, I could have lived with him now.

You say he mistook the love of virtue for the practice. I think that you have endeavoured to separate cause and effect. No cause do I esteem so indissolubly annexed to its effect as the real sincere love of virtue to the disinterested practice of its dictates. You seem to have confounded love of virtue with *talking* of the love of virtue. Yet was not his conduct most nobly disinterested at Oxford? This appeared real love of virtue. Then what a fall! But not a remediless one. How are we to tell a tree? Not even by its fruits. Are changes possible so quick, so sudden? I am immersed in a labyrinth of doubt. My friend, I need your advice, your reason: my own seems almost withered.

Will you come here in your Christmas holidays? Harriet delights so much in this place that I do not think I *can* quit it. Will you come here? The poison-blast of calumny will not dare to infect you. Besides, what is the world? Eliza Westbrook is here: it is not likely, therefore, that anything would be said.

We will never part in spirit: we are

too firmly convinced of what we
are ever to fear failure. Let the Christian talk of faith, but I am convinced
that the wildest bigot who ever carried
fury and fanaticism through a country
never could so firmly believe his idol
as I believe in you. Be you but false,
and I have no more to accomplish :
my usefulness is ended.

You talk of religion,—the influence
human depravity gained over your
mind towards acceding to it. But,
for this purpose, the religion of the
deist or the worshiper of virtue would
suffice, without involving the persecu-
tion, battles, bloodshed, which counten-
ancing Christianity countenances. I
think, my friend, *we* are the devoutest
professors of *true* religion I know,—if
the perverted and prostituted name of
" religion " is applicable to the idea of
devotion to virtue.

"The just man made perfect" I
doubt not of : but to this simple truth

where is the necessity of answering
fifty contradictory dogmas, in order
that men may destroy each other to
know which is right? You see even
now I can write against Christianity,
"the enormous faith of many made
for one."

I write this hasty letter by return of
post, because I do not wish to excite
the anxiety you name: it is a terrible
feeling.

My friend, my dearest friend, adieu.
One blessing has Fate given, to coun-
terpoise all the evil she has thrown
into my balance; and, when I cease to
estimate this blessing—a true, dear
friend—may I cease to live!

Your true, sincere, affectionate,

PERCY SHELLEY.

LETTER XVII.

KESWICK,

Nov. 23, 1811—SATURDAY.

MY DEAREST FRIEND,

Your letter reached me one day too late, on account of a tempest happening, and delaying the mail. It hath at length reached me ; and dear, sacredly dear, to me is every line of it. I feel as if this occurrence had deprived me of the breath of life which now with such eagerness I inhale. Oh friendship like ours ! its most soul-lulling comforts can, ought, never to be called selfish ; for, although we give each other pleasure, our love is not selfish. Reasoning is necessary to selfishness ; and the delight I feel in bracing my mind with the energies of yours is involuntary. It is the remote

result of reason ; but, in cases of this
nature, it is necessary that a pleasure
should immediately arise from the cool
calculation of degree of benefit resulting to itself, before it can be called
selfishness. Your letter has soothed,
tranquillized me : it seems as if every
bitter disappointment had changed its
bitter character.

I could have borne to die, to die
eternally, with my once-loved friend.
I could coolly have reasoned : to the
conclusions of reason I could have un-
hesitatingly submitted. Earth seemed
to be enough for our intercourse : on
earth its bounds appeared to be stated,
as the event hath dreadfully proved.
But with *you*—your friendship seems
to have generated a passion to which
fifty such fleeting inadequate existences
as these appear to be but the drop in
the bucket, too trivial for account.
With you, I cannot submit to perish
like the flower of the field. I cannot

consent that the same shroud which
shall moulder around these perishing
frames shall enwrap the vital spirit
which hath produced, sanctified—may
I say, eternized?—a friendship such
as ours. Most high and noble feelings
are referable to passion : but these—
these are referable to reason (certainly
"inspiration" hath nothing to do with
the latter). I say, passion is referable
to reason : but I mean the great aspir-
ing passions of disinterested Friendship, Philanthropy. It is necessary
that reason should disinterestedly determine : the passion of the virtuous
will then energetically put its decrees
in execution.

Your fancy does not run away with
your reason ; but your too great de-
pendence on mine does. Preserve
your individuality; reason for yourself;
compare and discuss with me, I will do
the same with you : for are you not
my second self, the stronger shadow of

that soul whose dictates I have been accustomed to obey?

I have taken a long *solitary* ramble to-day. These gigantic mountains piled on each other, these water-falls, these million-shaped clouds tinted by the varying colours of innumerable rainbows hanging between yourself and a lake as smooth and dark as a plain of polished jet—oh, these are sights attunable to the contemplation! I have been much struck by the grandeur of its imagery. Nature here sports in the awful waywardness of her solitude. The summits of the loftiest of these immense piles of rock seem but to elevate Skiddaw and Helvellyn. Imagination is resistlessly compelled to look back upon the myriad ages whose silent change placed them here; to look back when perhaps this retirement of peace and mountain-simplicity was the pandemonium of druidical imposture, the scene of Roman pollution, the resting-place of the savage denizen of these solitudes with the wolf.—Still, still further. Strain thy reverted fancy when no rocks, no lakes, no cloud-soaring mountains, were here ; but a vast, populous and licentious city stood in the midst of an immense plain. Myriads. flocked towards it. London itself scarcely exceeds it in the variety, the extensiveness of its corruption. Perhaps ere Man had lost reason, and lived an happy, happy race : no tyranny, no priestcraft, no war.— Adieu to the dazzling picture !

I have been thinking of you and of human nature. Your letter has been the partner of my solitude,—or rather I have not been alone, for you have been with me. Ought I to grieve? I? and hath not Fate been more than kind to me? Did I expect her to lavish on me the inexhaustible stores of her munificence? Yet hath she not done so? What right have I to

lament, to accuse her of barbarity?
Hath she not given *you* to me? Oh
how pityful ought all her other boons,
how contemptible ought all her inju-
ries, *now* to be considered! and you
to share my sorrows! Oh am I not
doubly now a wretch to cherish them?
I will tear them from my remembrance.
I cannot be gay—gaiety is not my
nature : I have seen too much ever to
be so. Yet I will be happy: and I
claim it as a sacred right too that you
should share my happiness. I will
not be *very long* at this distance from
you.

I transcribe a little poem I found
this morning. It was written some
time ago ; but, as it appears to show
what I then thought of eternal life, I
send it.

TO MARY,

WHO DIED IN THIS OPINION.

Maiden, quench the glare of sorrow
  Struggling in thine haggard eye :
Firmness dare to borrow
  From the wreck of destiny ;
For the ray morn's bloom revealing
  Can never boast so bright an hue
As that which mocks concealing,
  And sheds its loveliest light on you.

Yet is the tie departed
  Which bound thy lovely soul to bliss ?
Has it left thee broken-hearted
  In a world so cold as this ?
Yet, though, fainting fair one,
  Sorrow's self thy cup has given,
Dream thou'lt meet thy dear one,
  Never more to part, in heaven.

Existence would I barter
  For a dream so dear as thine,
And smile to die a martyr
  On affection's bloodless shrine.

Nor would I change for pleasure
That withered hand and ashy cheek,
If my heart enshrined a treasure
Such as forces thine to break.

Pardon me for thus writing on. I
preserve no connexion : I do not
hesitate, I do not pause one moment,
in writing to you. It seems to me as
if some spirit guided my pen.

I feel with you. I *will* stifle all
these idle regrets. I will sympathize
with you. Write to me your sensations, your feelings : ah, I fear I have
monopolized them ! Would that this
terrible sensation had not forced me
to call them thus into action ! But to
share grief is a sacred right of friendship—to share every thought, every
idea. Remember, this is a *sacred right.*
But why need I remind you of what
neither of us is in any danger of
forgetting ?

Harriet will write to you : I have

persuaded her. May she not share
the sunshine of my life ? O lovely sympathy ! thou art indeed life's sweetest,
only solace ! and is not my friend the
shrine of sympathy ?

I hear nothing of my temporal
affairs. The D[uke] of N[orfolk] hath
written to me : I have answered his
letter. He is polite enough. In truth,
I do not covet any ducal intercourse
or interference. I suppose this is
inevitable and necessary.

I have not seen Southey : he is not
now at Keswick. Believe that, on his
return, I will not be slow to pay
homage to a *really* great man.

Oh I have much, much to say ! Methinks words can scarcely embody ideas:
how wretchedly inadequate are letters !

Adieu, dearest of friends. Never do
I for a moment forget how eternally,
sincerely, I am

Yours,

Percy S.

Your letters are six days in coming.
Perhaps one of those hateful Sundays
has been envious of my solace.

LETTER XVIII.

KESWICK, CUMBERLAND,
Sunday, Nov. 24, 1811.

I ANSWER your letter, my dearest
Friend, not by return of post, because
the Keswick post comes in at seven and
goes out at nine, and we are some
distance.

Your letters revive me : they resus-
citate my slumbering hopes. The
languid flame of life, which before
burns feebly, glows at communication
with that vivid spark of friendship.
" Love " I do not think is so adequate
a sign of the idea : its usual signification involves selfish monopoly, the
sottish idiotism of frenzy-nourished
fools, as once I was. But let that era
be blotted from the memory of my
shame, when purity, truth, reason,
virtue, all sanctify a friendship which

shall endure when the "love" of common souls shall sleep where the shroud
moulders around their soulless bodies.
—What a rhapsody! But with you I
feel half inspired; and *then* feel half
ashamed, lest my inspiration, like that
of others, result [not] from a little
vanity.

I am discouraged. His letters of
late appear to me to betray *cunning*,
deep cunning. But I may be deceived: oh that I were in all that
these five weeks had brought forth!
His letters are long; but they never express any conviction or unison. They
appear merely calculated to bring about
what he calls "intimacy on the same
happy terms as formerly." This I
have positively forbade the very thought
of. I tell him that I am open to reason,—I wish, ardently wish, that he
would reason sincerely; but that, were
even convinced that his conduct re-
sulted from *disinterested* love of virtue,

he could not live with us, as I should thereby barter Harriet's happiness for his short-lived pleasure, — since, my friend, if it is true that *such* passions are unconquerable (which I do not believe), how much greater ascendency will they gain when under the immediate influence of their original excitement !

Love of what? Not love of my wife, for love seeks the happiness of its object, *even* when combined with the common-place infatuation of novels and gay life (oh no! I don't know that). Love of self; aye, as genuine and complete as the most bigoted believer in original sin could desire to defile mankind,—these *fine suscepti-bilities*, to which casual deformity and advanced age are such wonderful cures and preventatives. But these have nothing to do with real love, with friendship. Suppose *your* frame were wasted by sickness, your brow covered

with wrinkles ; suppose age had bowed
your form till it reached the ground,
would you not be as lovely as now?
Yet one of *these* beings would pass
that intellect, that soul, that sensibility, with as much indifference as I
would show to the night-star of a ball-
room, the magnet of the apes, asses,
geese, its inhabitants. So much for
real [? false] and so much for true
love. The one perishes with the body
whence on earth it never dares to soar ;
the other lives with the soul which was
the exclusive object of its homage.
Oh if this last be but true !

You talk of a future state : "is not
this imagination," you ask, "a proof of
it?" To me it appears so : to me
everything proves it. But what we
earnestly desire we are very much
prejudiced in favour of. It seems to
me that everything lives again.—What
is the Soul ? Look at yonder flower.
The blast of the North sweeps it from

the earth ; it withers beneath the breath of the destroyer. Yet that flower hath a soul : for what is soul but that which makes an organized being to be what it is,—without which it would not be so ? On this hypo- thesis, must not that (the soul) without which a flower cannot be a flower exist, when the earthly flower hath perished ? Yet where does it exist— in what state of being ? Have not flowers also some end which Nature destines their being to answer ? Doubt- less, it ill becomes us to deny this because we cannot certainly discover it ; since so many analogies seem to favour the probability of this hypo- thesis. I will say, then, that all Na- ture is animated ; that microscopic vision, as it hath discovered to us millions of animated beings whose pur- suits and passions are as eagerly fol- lowed as our own ; so might it, if extended, find that Nature itself was but a mass of organized animation. Perhaps the animative intellect of all this is in a constant rotation of change: perhaps a future state is no other than a different mode of terrestrial existence to which we have fitted ourselves in *this* mode.

Is there any probability in this supposition? On this plan, *congenial* souls must meet; because, having fitted themselves for nearly the same mode of being, they cannot fail to be *near* each other. Free-will must give energy to this infinite mass of being, and thereby constitute Virtue. If *our* change be in this mortal life, do not fear that we shall be among the grovelling souls of heroes, aristocrats, and commercialists.—Adieu to this.

I have scribbled a great deal: all my feeling, all my ideas as they arise, are thus yours. My dear friend, believe that thou art the cheering beam which gilds this wintry day of life,—

perhaps ere long to be the exhaustless sun which shall gild my millenniums of immortality.

Adieu, my dearest friend.

Ever, ever yours,

PERCY S.

LETTER XIX.

Keswick, Cumberland.
[*Tuesday*, 26 *November*, 1811.]

Your letters are like angels sent from heaven on missions of peace. They assure me that existence is not valueless; they point out the path which it is paradise to tread. And yet, my dearest friend, I am not satisfied that we should be so far asunder. Methinks letters are but imperfect pictures of the mind. They give the permanent and energic outline, but a thousand minutiæ of varied expressions are omitted in the portraiture. I am therefore sorry that you cannot come *now*. Cannot the sweet little nurslings of liberty come? But I will not press you.

Strange prejudices have these country people! I must relate one very singular one. The other night I was explaining to Harriet and Eliza the nature of the atmosphere; and, to illustrate my theory, I made some experiments on hydrogen gas, one of its constituent parts. This was in the garden, and the vivid flame was seen at some distance. A few days after, Mr. Dare entered our cottage, and said he had something to say to me. "Why, sir," said he, "I am not satisfied with you. I wish you to leave my house." "Why, sir?" "Because the country talks very strangely of your proceedings. Odd things have been seen at night near your dwelling. I am very ill satisfied with this. Sir, I don't like to talk of it: I wish you to provide yourself elsewhere."—I have, with much difficulty, quieted Mr. D.'s fears. He does not, however, much like us; and I am by no means certain that he will permit us to remain.

Have *you* found a house? I have

your promise: next Midsummer will
be my holidays. Heaven ! were I the
charioteer of Time, his burning wheels
would rapidly attain the goal of my
aspirations.

You believe, firmly believe me.
How invaluably dear ought *now* to be
that credit, when an example so terrible has warned you to be sceptical !
That I believe in you cannot be wonderful, for the first words you spoke to
me, the manner, are eternal earnests of
your taintlessness and sincerity. But
wherefore do I talk thus, when we
know, feel, each other ; when every sentiment is reciprocal ; when congeniality,
so often laughed at, both have found
proof strong as internal evidence can
afford ?

I do not love him now: bear witness for me, thou reciprocity of thought,
that I do not ! It is, it is true—too
true : what you say is conclusive. It
tallies too well with what I have yet to

tell you. Oh I have been fearfully deceived! It is not the degradation of imposition that I lament; but that a character moulded, as I imagined, in all the symmetry of virtue, should exhibit the loathsome deformity of vice— that a saviour should change to a destroyer.—But adieu to that now.

I shall not accuse my friend of endeavouring to insinuate the tenets of a religion in one sentence, the foundation, the corner-stone, of which she defies all the powers that exist to make her believe, in the next.

Miss Weeke's marriage induces you to think marriage an evil. *I* think it an evil—an evil of immense and extensive magnitude: but I think a previous reformation in myself—and that a general and a great one—is requisite before it may be remedied. Man is the creature of circumstances; and these, casual circumstances, custom hath made unto him a second nature.

That which hath no more to do with
virtue than the most indifferent actions
of our lives hath been exalted into its
criterion ; and, from being *considered*
so, hath *become* one of its criterions.
Marriage is monopolizing, exclusive,
jealous. The tie which binds it bears
the same relation to "friendship in
which excess is lovely" that the body
doth to the soul. Everything which
relates simply to this clay-formed dun-
geon is comparatively despicable ; and,
in a state of perfectible society, could
not be made the subject of either
virtue or vice. The most delicious
strains of music, viands the most titil-
lating to the palate, wines of the most
exquisite flavour, if it be innocent to
derive delight from them (supposing
such a case), it surely must be as innocent in whosesoever company it were
derived. A law to compel you to
hear this music, in the company of
such a particular person, appears to me

parallel to that of marriage. Were there even now such a law as this, were this exclusiveness reckoned the criterion of virtue, it certainly would not be worth the while of rational people to "offend their weak brothers" (as St. Paul says) "by eating meats placed before the idols." It ill would become them to risk the peace of others, however prejudiced, by gaining to themselves what from their souls they hold in contempt.

Am I right? It delights me to discuss and to be sceptical : thus we must arrive at truth — that introducer of virtue and usefulness.

Have you read Godwin's *Enquirer* (1)—his *St. Leon* (2)—his *Political Justice* (3)—his *Caleb Williams* (4)?— 1 is very good ; 2 is good, very good ; 3 is long, sceptical, good ; 4 is good. I put them in the order that I would advise you to read them.

I understand you when you say we are free. Liberty is the very soul of friendship, and from the very soul of liberty art thou my friend ; aye, and such a sense as this can never fade.

> "Earthly those passions of the earth
> Which perish where they had their birth,
> But Love is indestructible."

I almost wish that Southey had not made the Glendover a male : these detestable distinctions will surely be abolished in a future state of being.

> "The holy flame for ever burneth :
> From heaven it came, to heaven returneth."

Might there not have been a prior state of existence? might we not have been friends then? The creation of soul at birth is a thing I do not like. Where we have no premisses, we can therefore draw no conclusions. It *may* be all vanity : but I cannot think so.

I may be in Sussex soon. I do not know where I shall be: but, wherever I am, I shall be with you in spirit and in truth. Do not think I am going to insinuate Christianity, though I think it is as likely a thing as that *you* should. I annihilate God; you destroy the Devil: and then we make a heaven entirely to our own mind. It must be owned that we are tolerably independent. As to your ghostly director, who told you to put out your sun of common sense in order that he might set up his rushlight, I can scarcely believe that he ever even imagined a " call."

When shall you change your abode? Are you fixed at Hurst for some years? I wish to know, as this will enable me to determine on some place of residence near to yours.

This country is heavenly: I will describe it when I have seen more of it. I wish to stay, too, to see Southey. You may imagine, then, that I was very humble to Mr. Dare: I should think he was tolerably afraid of the devil.

I have heard from Hogg since, often :

his letters give me little hope. He
still earnestly desires to live with us.
You have brought me into a dilemma,
concerning his conduct, from which it
is impossible to escape. I do not
love him. I have examined his conduct, I hope with cool impartiality;
and I grieve to find the conclusion
thus unfavourable.

I hope you are indebted (as you call
it) to the coolness of my judgment for
my opinion of you. I have repeatedly
told you what I think of you. I consider you one of those beings who
carry happiness, reform, liberty, wherever they go. To me you are as my
better genius—the judge of my reasonings, the guide of my actions, the
influencer of my usefulness. Great
responsibility is the consequence of
high powers.

I am, as you must be, a despiser of
the mock-modesty of the world, which
is accustomed to conceal more defects

than excellencies. I know I am superior to the mob of mankind : but I
am inferior to you in everything but
the equality of friendship.

But my paper ends. Adieu. I bid
adieu to-day to what is to me inexpressibly dear, your society.

Ever yours unalterably,

PERCY S.

Tuesday morning. On what day
does this letter reach you ?

Harriet desires me to send her love,
and hopes you will answer her letter
very soon.

LETTER XX.

[KESWICK.

Monday, 9 *December,* 1811?]

MY DEAREST FRIEND,

I have just found your letters.
Three of them were here on our return
from Greystoke. What will you think
of not hearing from me so long? Not
that I have forgotten you. Your
letters were indeed a most valuable
treasure. I have just finished reading
them. I shall answer them to-morrow.

We met several people at the Duke's.
One in particular struck me. He was
an elderly man, who seemed to know
all my concerns; and the expression
of his face, whenever I held the arguments, which I do *everywhere*, was such
as I shall not readily forget. I shall

have more to tell of him, for we have met him before in these mountains, and his particular look then struck Harriet.

Adieu, my dearest friend. I am compelled to break off in the middle of my letter by the conviction that this *may* be too late. You will hear from me to-morrow.

Yours, ever yours,

PERCY SHELLEY.

LETTER XXI.

KESWICK, CUMBERLAND.

[*Tuesday,* 10 *December,* 1811.]

YOU received a fleeting letter from me yesterday. An immediate acknowledgement of your letters I judged equal in value to the postage of a blank sheet of paper.

Your letters, my dearest friend, are to me an exhaustless mine of pleasure. Fatigued with aristocratical insipidity, left alone scarce one moment by those senseless monopolizers of time that form the court of a Duke, who would be very well as a man, how delightful to commune with the soul which is undisguised—whose importance no arts are necessary nor adequate to exalt !

I admire your father, but I do not think him capable of sympathizing with you. I, you know, consider mind to be the creature of education : that, in proportion to the characters thereon impressed by circumstance or intention, so does it assume the appearances which vary with these varying events. Divest every event of its improper tendency, and evil becomes annihilate. Thus, then, I am led to love a being, not because it stands in the physical relation of blood to me, but because I discern an intellectual relationship. It is because chance. hath placed us in a situation most fit for rendering happiness to our relations that, if higher considerations intervene not, makes it our duty to devote ourselves to this object. This is your duty, and nobly do you fulfil it. Your father, I plainly see, has some mistakes. Cannot you reason him out of that rough exterior ? It has the semblance of sincerity : in reality is it not deceit ? Your attention to his happiness is at once so noble, so delicate, so desirous of accomplishing its design, that how could he fail, if he knew it, to give you that esteem and respect, besides the love which he does? Methinks he is not your equal —that I have not found you equalled. Were he so, would he not discern your attentions? No : he must be like you, before I can ever institute a comparison between your characters.

Of your mother I have not much opinion. She appears to me one of those every-day characters by whom the stock of prejudice is augmented rather than decreased.

Obedience (were society as I could wish it) is a word which ought to be without meaning. If virtue depended on duty, then would prudence be virtue, and imprudence vice; and the only difference between the Marquis Wellesley and William Godwin would be that the latter had more cunningly devised the means of his own benefit. This cannot be. Prudence is only an auxiliary of virtue, by which it may become useful. Virtue consists in the motive. Paley's *Moral Philosophy* begins : " Why am I *obliged* to keep my word ? Because I desire heaven, and hate hell." Obligation and duty, therefore, are words of no value as the criterion of excellence.—So much for obedience—parents and children. Do you agree to my definition of Virtue —" Disinterestedness ? "—Why do I enquire ?

I am as little inclined as you are to quarrel with Taffy : I am as much obliged to him for the complex idea, Tyranny. You do understand Locke. This is one of his "complex ideas." The ideas of power, evil, pain, together with a very clear perception of the two latter which may almost define the idea " hatred," together with other minor ideas, enter into its composition.

What you say about residing near you is true. We cannot either get a

house there immediately. At midsummer, perhaps before, we see you
here: that is certain. Oh how you
will delight in this scenery! These
mountains are now capped with snow.
The lake, as I see it hence, is glassy
and calm. Snow-vapours, tinted by
the loveliest colours of refraction, pass
far below the summits of these giant
rocks. The scene, even in a winter
sunset, is inexpressibly lovely. The
clouds assume shapes which seem pe-
culiar to these regions. What will it
be in summer? What when *you* are
here? Oh give me a little cottage in
that scene! Let all live in peaceful
little houses—let temples and palaces
rot with their perishing masters! Be
society civilized; be you with us;
grant eternal life to all; and I will ask
not the paradise of religionists! I
think the Christian heaven (with its
hell) would be to *us* no paradise: but
such a scene as this!

How my pen runs away with me !—
We design, after your visit (which
Heaven knows, I wish would *never*
end), to visit Ireland.   We are very
near Port-Patrick.   If you could ex-
tend your time, could *you* not accom-
pany us ?   But am I not building on a
foundation more flimsy than air ?   Can
I look back to the last year, and decide
with certainty on anything but the
eternity of my regard for *you ?*

Every day augments the strength of
my friendship for you, dearest friend.
Every day makes me feel more keenly
that our being is eternal.   Every day
brings the conviction how futile, how
inadequate, are all reasonings to de-
monstrate it ?   Yet are we—are these
souls which measure in their circum-
scribed domain the distance of yon
orbs—are we but bubbles which arise
from the filth of a stagnant pool, merely
to be again re-absorbed into the mass
of its corruption ?   I think not : I feel

not. Can you prove it? Yet the
eternity of man has ever been believed.
It is not merely one of the dogmas of
an inconsistent religion, though all religions have taken it for their foundation.
The wild American, who never heard
of Christ, or dreamed of original sin,
whose " Great Spirit " was nothing but
the Soul of Nature, could not reconcile
his feelings to annihilation. He too
has his paradise. And in truth is not
the Iroquois's " human life perfected "
better than to "circle with harps the
golden throne " of one who dooms half
of his creatures to eternal destruction ?
—Thus much for the Soul.

I have now, my dear friend, in contemplation a poem. I intend it to be
by anticipation a picture of the manners,
simplicity, and delights of a perfect state
of society, though still earthly. Will
you assist me? I only thought of it
last night. I design to accomplish it,
and publish. After, I shall draw a

picture of Heaven.   I can do neither
without some hints from you.   The
latter I think you ought to *make*.

I told you of a strange man I met
the other day: I am going to see him.
I shall also see Southey, Wordsworth,
and Coleridge, there.   I shall then give
you a picture of them. ⸴

I owe you several letters, nor shall I
be slack to pay you.   I even now have
much—oh, much!—to say.   But never
can I express the abundance of pleasure
which your three letters have given me.
Surely, my dearest friend, you must
have known by intuition all my thoughts
to write me as you have done.

Give my love to Anne: what does
she think of me?   You delight me by
what you tell me of her.   Every prejudice conquered, every error rooted out,
every virtue given, is so much gained
in the cause of reform.   I am never
unmindful of this: I see that you are
not.   Tell Anne that if she would

write to me, I would answer her letters.

Now, my dearest friend, adieu. This paper is at an end, but what I have to say is not. I owe you several letters, and shall not fail in the payment.

What think you of my undertaking? Shall I not get into prison? Harriet is sadly afraid that his Majesty will provide me with a lodging, in consideration of the zeal which I evince for the bettering of his subjects.

I think I shall also make a selection of my younger poems for publication. You will give me credit for their morality.

Well, adieu, my dearest friend—thou to whom every thought, every shade of thought, is owing, since last I wrote. Adieu.

Your sincerest,

PERCY S.

Harriet sends her love to you : the dear girl will write to you.

LETTER XXII.

KESWICK, [CUMBERLAND.]
Sunday, December 15 [1811].

MY DEAREST FRIEND,

You will before now have my last letter. I have felt the distrustful recurrences of the post-office, which *you* felt when no answer to all your letters came. I have regretted that visit to Greystoke, because this delay must have given you uneasiness.

I have since heard from Captain P. His letter contains the account of a meditated proposal, on the part of my father and grandfather, to make my income immediately larger than the former's, in case I will consent to entail the estate on my eldest son, and, in default of issue, on my brother. Silly dotards ! do they think I can be thus bribed and ground into an act of such contemptible injustice and inutility? that I will forswear my principles in consideration of £2000 a year? that the good-will I could thus purchase, or the ill-will I could thus overbear, would recompense me for the loss of self-esteem, of conscious rectitude? And with what face can they make to me a proposal so insultingly hateful? Dare one of them propose such a condition to my face—to the face of any virtuous man—and not sink into nothing at his disdain? That I should entail £120,000 of command over labour, of power to remit this, to employ it for beneficient purposes, on one whom I know not—who might, instead of being the benefactor of mankind, be its bane, or use this for the worst purposes, which the real delegates of my chance-given property might convert into a most useful instrument of benevolence! —No! this *you* will not suspect me of.

What I have told you will serve to
put in its genuine light the grandeur of
aristocratical distinctions; and to show
that contemptible vanity will gratify its
unnatural passion at the expense of
every just, humane, and philanthropic
consideration,—

> "Though to a radiant angel linked
> Will sate itself in a celestial bed,
> And prey on garbage."

I have written this to you just as I
have received the Captain's letter. My
indignant contempt has probably con-
fused my language, and rendered my
writing rather illegible. But it is my
custom to communicate to you, my
dearest friend,—to that brain of sym-
pathetic sensibility—every idea as it
comes, as I do to my own.

Hogg at length has declared himself
to be one of those mad votaries of
selfishness who are cool to destroy the

peace of others, and revengeful, when
their schemes are foiled, even to idiotism. In answer to a letter in which
I strongly insisted on the criminality of
exposing himself to the inroads of a
passion which he had proved himself
unequal to control, and endangering
Harriet's happiness, he has talked of
my "consistency in despising religion,
despising duelling, and despising sincere friendship"—with some hints as
to duelling, to induce me to meet him
in that manner. I have answered his
letter; in which I have said I shall not
fight a duel with him, whatever he may
say or do; that I have no right either
to expose my own life, or take his—in
addition to the wish I have, from
various motives, to prolong my exist-
tence. Nor do I think that his life is
a fair exchange for mine; since I have
acted up to my principles, and he has
denied his, and acted inconsistently
with any morality whatsoever. That,

if he would show how I had wronged him, I would repair it to the uttermost mite; but I would not fight a duel.

Now, dearest partner of that friendship which once *he* shared, now I am at peace. He is incapable of being other but the every-day villain who parades St. James's Street; though even as a villain will he be eminent and imposing. The chances are now much against *my* ever influencing him to adopt habits of benevolence and philanthropy. This passion of animal love which has seized him, this which the false refinements of society have exalted into an idol to which its misguided members burn incense, has intoxicated him, and rendered him incapable of being influenced by any but the consideration of self-love. How much worthier of a rational being is friendship! which, though it wants none of the " impassionateness " which

some have characterized as the inseparable of the other, yet retains judgment, which is not blind though it
may chance to see something like
perfections in its object, which retains its sensibility, but whose sensibility is celestial and intellectual,
unallied to the grovelling passions of
the earth.

Southey has changed. I shall see
him soon, and I shall reproach him
for his tergiversation. He, to whom
bigotry, tyranny, law were hateful, has
become the votary of these idols in a
form the most disgusting. The Church
of England—its Hell and all—has become the subject of his panegyric. The
war in Spain, that prodigal waste of
human blood to aggrandize the fame of
statesmen, is his delight. The constitu-
tion of England—with its Wellesley, its
Paget, and its Prince—is inflated with
the prostituted exertions of his pen. I
feel a sickening distrust when I see all

that I had considered good, great, or imitable, fall around me into the gulf of error. But *we* will struggle on its brink to the last ; and, if compelled we fall, we shall have at all events the consolation of knowing that we *have* struggled with a nature that is bad, and that this nature—not the imbecility of our proper cowardice—has involved us in the ignominy of defeat.

Wordsworth, a *quondam* associate of Southey, yet retains the integrity of his independence ; but his poverty is such that he is frequently obliged to beg for a shirt to his back.

Well, dearest friend, adieu. Changes happen, friends fall around us: what once *was* great sinks into the imbecility of human grandeur. Empires shall fade, kings shall be peasants, and peasants shall be kings: but never will *we* cease to regard each other, because we never will cease to deserve it.

My Harriet desires her love to you.

Yours most *imperishably*, and eternally,

P. B. SHELLEY.

I shall write again. Do these letters come as a single sheet?

LETTER XXIII.

Keswick, [Cumberland,
Thursday,] *December* 26, 1811.

My dearest Friend,

I have delayed writing for two days, that my letters might not succeed each other so closely as one day. I have also been engaged in talking with Southey. You may conjecture that a man must possess high and estimable qualities if, with the prejudices of such total difference from my sentiments, I can regard him great and worthy. In fact, Southey is an advocate of liberty and equality. He looks forward to a state when all shall be perfected, and matter become subjected to the omnipotence of mind. But he is now an advocate for existing establishments. He says he designs his three statues in

Kehama to be contemplated with republican feelings, but not in this age. Southey hates the Irish : he speaks against Catholic Emancipation, and Parliamentary Reform. In these things we differ, and our differences were the subject of a long conversation. Southey calls himself a Christian ; but he does not believe that the Evangelists were inspired ; he rejects the Trinity, and thinks that Jesus Christ stood precisely in the same relation to God as himself. Yet he calls himself a Christian. Now, if ever there were a definition of a Deist, I think it could never be clearer than this confession of faith. But Southey, though far from being a man of great reasoning powers, is a great man. He has all that characterizes the poet,—great eloquence, though obstinacy in opinion, which arguments are the last thing that can shake. He is a man of virtue. He will never belie what he thinks ; his professions are in

strict compatibility with his practice.—
More of him another time.

With Calvert, the man whom I mentioned to you in that pygmy letter, we
have now become acquainted. He
knows everything that relates to my
family and myself : my expulsion from
Oxford, the opinions that caused it, are
no secrets to him. We first met Southey
at his house. He has been very kind
to us. The rent of our cottage was
two guineas and a half a week, with
linen provided : he has made the pro-
prietor lower it to one guinea, and has
lent us linen himself. We are likely
therefore to continue where we are, as
we have engaged, on these terms, for
three months. After that, we will
augment his rent.

Believe me, my most valued friend,
that I am, no less than yourself, an ad-
mirer of sincerity and openness. Mystery is hateful and foreign to all my
habits : I wish to have no reserves.

Were the world composed of such individuals as that which shares my soul, it should be the keeper of my conscience. But I do not know whether, in the first place, the circumstance of Hogg's apostacy is such as would in any wise contribute to benefit by its publication; and, *not* knowing this, should I not be highly criminal to risk anything by its disclosure? Though I have much respect and love for my uncle and aunt, and indeed can never be sufficiently thankful for their unlimited kindness, yet I know that no good end, save explicitness, is to be answered by this explanation; and my uncle's indignation would be so great that I have frequently pictured to myself the possibility of [its] outstepping the limits of justice. My aunt, too, would be voluble in resentment; and I am conscious that she suspected, long before its event, the occurrence of this terrible disappointment.

To you I tell everything that passes in my soul, even the secret thoughts sacred alone to sympathy. But you are my *dearest* friend ; and, so long as the present system of things continues (which I fear is not yet verging to its demolition), so long must some distinction be established between those for whom you have a great esteem, a high regard, and those who are to you what Eliza Hitchener is to me.

Since I have answered Hogg's letter, I have received another. It was not written until after the receipt of my answer. Its strain is humble and compliant : he talks of his quick passions, his high sense of honour. I have not answered it, nor shall I. He has too deeply plunged into hypocrisy for *my* arguments to effect any change. I leave him to his fate. Would that I could have reached him ! It is an unavailing wish—the last one that I shall breathe over departed excellence.

How I have loved him *you* can feel.
But he is no longer the being whom
perhaps 'twas the warmth of my imagination that pictured. I love no
longer what is not that which I loved.

Do not praise me so much: my
counsellor will overturn the fabric she
is erecting. You strengthen me in
virtue : but weaken not the energy of
your example by proposing your so
high esteem as a reward for acting well.
I know none, of my principles, who
would do otherwise.

This proposal will be (if made) a
proof of the imbecility of aristocracy.
I have been led into reasonings which
make me hate more and more the
existing establishment, of every kind.
I gasp when I think of plate and balls
and titles and kings. I have beheld
scenes of misery. The manufacturers
are reduced to starvation. My friends
the military are gone to Nottingham.
Curses light on them for their motives,

if they destroy one of its famine-wasted inhabitants ! But, if I were a friend to the destroyed, myself about to perish, I fancy that I could bless them for saving my friend the bitter mockery of a trial. Southey thinks that a revolution is *inevitable :* this is one of his reasons for supporting things as they are. But let *us* not belie our principles. They may feed and may riot and may sin to the last moment. The groans of the wretched may pass unheeded till the latest moment of this infamous revelry, —till the storm burst upon them, and the oppressed take ruinous vengeance on the oppressors.

I do not proceed with my poem : the subject is not now to my mind. I am composing some essays which I design to publish in the summer. The minor poems I mentioned you will see soon : they are about to be sent to the printers. I think it wrong to publish anything anonymously, and shall annex my name, and a preface in which I shall lay open my intentions, as the poems are not wholly useless.

"I sing, and Liberty may love the song."

Can you assist my graver labours?

Harriet complains that I hurt my health, and fancies that I shall get into prison. The dear girl sends her love to you : she is quite what is called "in love" with you.

What do you advise me about Hogg and my uncle? If you think best, I will tell him. Do you be my mentor, my guide, my counsellor, the half of my soul : I demand it.

I never heard of Parkinson. I have not room to say anything of Xenophanes. I shall send for the *Organic Remains*, &c. You will like the *Political Justice :* for its politics you are prepared. I hope you have got the *first* edition. The chapters on Truth and sincerity are impressively true.— But I anticipate your opinions.

I have neglected ten thousand things
—in my next.

I *will* live beyond this life.

Yours, yours most imperishably,

PERCY S.

If they charge you a double sheet show this,* or open it before them, and they will retract.

* Marked outside : " This is *only* a large single sheet."

LETTER XXIV.

KESWICK, [CUMBERLAND,
Thursday,] *Jan.* 2, 1812.

MY DEAREST FRIEND,

YOUR immense sheet, and the voluminousness of your writing, and my pleasure, demand an equivalent. I can give it at length : but do not flatter me so much as to suppose that I can equal you in interest. Your style may not be so polished ; sometimes I think it is not so legal as mine : but words are only signs of ideas, and their arrangement only valuable as it is adapted adequately to express them. Your eloquence comes from the soul : it has the impassionateness of nature. I sometimes doubt the source of mine, and suspect the genuineness of my sincerity. But I do not think I have any reason : no, I am firm, secure, unchangeable.—Pardon this scepticism ; but I will incorporate, for the inspection of my second conscience, each shadow, however fleeting, each idea which worth or chance imprints on my recollection.

You have loved God, but not the God of Christianity. A God of pardons and revenge, a God whose will could change the order of the universe, seems never to have been the object of your affections. I have lately had some conversation with Southey which has elicited my true opinions of God. He says I ought not to call myself an atheist, since in reality I believe that the Universe is God. I tell him I believe that " God " is another signification for " the Universe." I then explain :—I think reason and analogy seem to countenance the opinion that life is infinite ; that, as the soul which now animates this frame was once the vivifying principle of the infinitely

lowest link in the chain of existence, so
is it ultimately destined to attain the
highest; that everything is animation
(as explained in my last letter); and in
consequence, being infinite, we can
never arrive at its termination. How,
on this hypothesis, are we to arrive at
a First Cause?—Southey admits and
believes this. Can he be a Christian?
Can God be three? Southey agrees in
my idea of Deity,—the mass of infinite
intelligence. I, you, and he, are constituent parts of this immeasurable
whole. What is now to be thought of
Jesus Christ's divinity? To me it
appears clear as day that it is the falsehood of human-kind.

You seem much to doubt Christianity. I do not: I cannot conceive in
my mind even the possibility of its genuineness. I am far from thinking you
weak and imbecile: you must know
this. I look up to you as a mighty
mind. I anticipate the era of reform

with the more eagerness as I picture to myself *you* the barrier between violence and renovation. Assert your true character, and believe one who loves you for what you are to be sincere. Knowing you to be thus great, I should grieve that you countenanced imposture. Love God, if thou wilt (I do not think you ever feared Him), but recollect what God is.

If what I have urged against Christianity is insufficient, read its very books, that a nearer inspection may contribute to the rectifying any false judgment. Physical considerations must not be disregarded, when physical improbabilities are asserted by the witnesses of a contested question. Bearing in mind that disinterestedness is the essence of virtuous motive, any dogmas militating with this principle are to be rejected. Considering that belief is not a voluntary operation of the mind, any system which makes it a subject of reward or punishment cannot be supposed to emanate from one who has a master-knowledge of the human mind. All investigations of the era of the world's existence are incongruous with that of Moses. Whether is it probable that Moses or Sir Isaac Newton, knew astronomy best? Besides, Moses writes the history of his own death; which is almost as extraordinary a thing to do as to describe the creation of the world. Thus much for Christianity. This only relates to the truth of it : do not forget the weightier consideration of its direct effects.

Southey is no believer in original sin : he thinks that which appears to be a taint of our nature is in effect the result of unnatural political institutions. There we agree. He thinks the prejudices of education, and sinister influences of political institutions, adequate to account for all the specimens of vice which have fallen within his observation.

You talk of Montgomery. We all sympathise with him, and often think and converse of him. I am going to write to him to-day. His story is a terrible one: it is briefly this.— His father and mother were Moravian missionaries. They left their country to convert the Indians: they were young, enthusiastic, and excellent. The Indians savagely murdered them. Montgomery was then quite a child; but the impression of this event never wore away. When he grew up, he became a disbeliever of Christianity, having very much such principles as a virtuous enquirer for truth. In the mean time he loved an apparently amiable female : he was about to marry her. Having some affairs in the West Indies, he went to settle them before his marriage. On his return to Sheffield, he actually met the marriage-procession of this woman, who had in the mean time chosen another love. He became

melancholy-mad : the horrible events
of his life preyed on his mind. He
was shocked at having forsaken a faith
for which a father and mother whom
he loved had suffered martyrdom
The contest between his reason and
his faith was destroying. He is now a
Methodist. Will not this tale account
for the melancholy and religious cast
of his poetry ?— This is what Southey
told me, word for word.

"POET'S EPITAPH.

"Art thou a Statesman, in the van
  Of public business born and bred ?
First learn to love one living man ;
  Then mayest thou think upon the
    dead.

"Art thou a lawyer ? Come not nigh :
  Go, carry to some other place
The hardness of thy coward eye,
  The falsehood of thy sallow face.

" Art thou a man of rosy cheer,
   A purple man right plump to sec?
Approach : but, Doctor, not too near !
   This grave no cushion is for thee.

" Physician art thou—one all eyes—
   Philosopher—a fingering slave—
One who would peep and botanize
   Upon his mother's grave?

" Wrapped closely in thy sensual fleece,
   Pass quickly on : and take, I pray,
That he below may rest in peace,
   Thy pin-point of a soul away.

*   *   *   *

" But who is he, with modest looks,
   And clad in homely russet—brown,
Who murmurs near the running brooks
   A music sweeter than their own?

" And you must love him, ere to you
   He will seem worthy of your love.

"All outward shows of sky and earth,
  Of sea and valley, he hath viewed ;
And impulses of deeper birth
  Have come to him in solitude."

I have transcribed a piece of
Wordsworth's poetry. It may give
you some idea of the man. How
expressively keen are the first stanzas !
I shall see this man soon.

I wish I knew your mother: I do
not mean your natural, but your moral,
mother. I have many thanks to give
to her. I owe her much : more than
I can hope to repay, yet not without
the reach of an attempt at remunera-
tion.

I look forward to the time when you
will *live* with us : I think you ought at
some time. If *then* principle still
directs you to take scholars, this will
be no impediment : but I think you
might be far more usefully employed.
Your pen—so overflowing, so demon-

strative, so impassioned—ought· to
trace characters for a nation's perusal,
and not make grammar-books for children. This latter is undoubtedly a
most useful employment: but who
would consent that *such* powers should
always be so employed? .This is, however, a subject for afterwards. .

My Poems will make .their. appearance as soon as I can find a· printer.
As to *the* poem, I have for the present
postponed its execution ;. thinking that,
if I can finish my Essays, and a Tale in
which I design to exhibit.the cause of
the failure of.the.French Revolution,
and the state.of morals and opinions
in France during the latter years of its
monarchy.* Some.of the leading passions of the human mind will of course
have a place in its fabric. I design· to
exclude the sexual passion ;· and think
the keenest satire on ·its intemperance
will be complete.silence on the subject.

* Shelley has left this sentence uncompleted.

I have already done about 200 pages of this work, and about 150 of the Essays.

Now, you can assist me, and you *do* assist me. I must censure my friend's inadequate opinion of herself; for truly inadequate must it be if it inequalizes our intellectual powers. Have confidence in yourself: dare to believe " I am great."

I fear you cannot read my crossed writing: indeed, I very much doubt whether the whole of my scribbling be not nearly illegible.

Adieu, my dearest friend. Harriet sends her love.

Eliza, her sister, is a very amiable girl. Her opinions are gradually rectifying ; and, although I have never spoken of her to you before, it is injustice to her to conceal [her] from you so long.

I have said nothing of Godwin— nothing of a thousand topics I had to write on. But I admire Godwin as

much as you can.   I shall write to him
too to-day or to-morrow.   I do not sup
pose that he will answer my address.   I
shall, however, call on him whenever I
go to London.

I am not sure that Southey is *quite*
uninfluenced by venality.   He is disinterested, so far as respects his family;
but I question if he is so, as far as respects the world.   His writings solely
support a numerous family.   His sweet
children are such amiable creatures that
I almost forgive what I suspect.   His
wife is very stupid: Mrs. Coleridge is
worse.   Mrs. Lovel, who was once an
actress, is the best of them.

Adieu, my friend and fellow-labourer;
and never think that I can be otherwise
than devoted to you till annihilation.

Yours for ever,

P. B. SHELLEY.

Southey says I am not an Atheist,
but a Pantheist.

www.ingramcontent.com/pod-product-compliance
Lightning Source LLC
Chambersburg PA
CBHW020008030726
47500CB00002B/498